STAR WARS

Betrayal at Bespin

Book Seven

DISNEY · LUCASFILM PRESS

Los Angeles • New York

Han Solo was on the run. He and Chewbacca were being chased by the evil Sith Lord Darth Vader. Vader wanted them for helping the rebels, including the rebel leader Princess Leia, who was on the ship with them.

The hyperdrive on the *Millennium Falcon* was broken, so Han guided the ship through an asteroid field. The Imperial ships fell behind, trying to dodge the asteroids. Han piloted the *Falcon* deep into a cave inside a huge asteroid. They would be able to hide there for a little while and repair the hyperdrive.

Han and Chewbacca got to work repairing the hyperdrive. Then the crew heard strange noises from outside the ship. Han, Chewie, and Leia went into the cave to investigate.

Suddenly, a swarm of pale, leathery creatures flew past them. Han recognized them as mynocks—pests that had a bad habit of chewing on starships' power cables. Just then, the cave began to shake.

"This is no cave," Han said. They had to get out of there!

Han and Chewie flew the *Falcon* toward the opening of the cave. As they emerged the cave snapped shut behind them . . . with a clash of teeth!

They had been inside the mouth of a giant space slug—and they had barely escaped it alive!

They had evaded the Imperial TIE fighters, but Han had to figure out what to do as the *Millennium Falcon* found itself facing an Imperial Star Destroyer. He desperately tried to maneuver the *Falcon* away from the Star Destroyer.

With nowhere else to go, Han decided to turn the *Falcon* around and fly straight toward the enemy ship. At the very last second, Han changed course and attached the *Falcon* to the back of the giant ship.

He hoped that the Star Destroyer would not be able to sense them so close. It was a risky move, but taking risks had worked for the rebels so far!

Han's plan worked! The Imperial fleet could not find the *Millennium Falcon* anywhere.

"They'll dump their garbage before they go to lightspeed," Han began, "then we just float away . . ."

"With the rest of the garbage," Princess Leia finished.

The Star Destroyer did just as Han had predicted. With a *whoosh*, the *Millennium Falcon* detached itself from the Imperial ship and hid in the Empire's floating garbage. But they didn't realize they were being watched

Han needed to find a safe place to repair the *Falcon*'s malfunctioning hyperdrive. Unfortunately, he wasn't just was trying to avoid Darth Vader; he was also on the run from the slimy gangster Jabba the Hutt. Han owed him—and many others—a lot of money. It seemed as if Han was running out of places in the galaxy to hide.

Then Han had an idea. He decided to fly to Bespin, where his old friend Lando Calrissian was an administrator. Han hadn't seen Lando in years, but he was sure that the former smuggler shared his dislike of the Empire.

When the *Millennium Falcon* landed, a smiling Lando welcomed them to Cloud City.

As Lando gave them a tour of Cloud City, C-3PO thought he heard the familiar whistle of an R2 unit. He broke off from the group to find the little droid but instead found a secret squadron of Imperial stormtroopers!

"I'm terribly sorry," C-3PO began. "I didn't mean to intrude." But it was too late. With one shot, C-3PO was scattered into a dozen pieces and tossed away.

Chewbacca noticed that C-3PO was missing and went to find him, but the protocol droid was nowhere in sight. The Wookiee moaned in frustration.

Chewbacca kept searching for C-3PO until he came to a junk room filled with spare parts. Ugnaughts—short hoglike creatures—were inspecting the junk. Chewbacca was surprised to see pieces of C-3PO mixed in with the spare parts. Chewbacca roared angrily and gathered all the pieces of his broken friend. He quickly took the parts back to Han and Leia.

Just then, Lando invited everyone to join him for some refreshments.

As Lando led the group to the dining hall, he told them that he had just made a deal that would keep the Empire out of Cloud City forever. Then the doors to the dining hall opened. At the far end of the grand banquet table was the most fearsome villain in the galaxy: Darth Vader.

Han drew his blaster and fired four quick blasts. But Vader held up his hand and effortlessly deflected them.

"We would be honored if you would join us," Vader said calmly as Boba Fett stepped into view.

Han, Leia, and Chewbacca were now prisoners of the Empire. Inside a cell, Chewbacca sat with the broken pieces of C-3PO. He attached the droid's head to his upper body. C-3PO sprang to life and recounted his last memory.

"Stormtroopers? Here?" C-3PO gasped. "We're in danger. I must tell the others." Chewie told him about Darth Vader.

Meanwhile, things were getting worse for Han. Boba Fett wanted to take the smuggler to his employer.

"You may take Captain Solo to Jabba the Hutt after I have Skywalker," Vader said.

Lando protested: he had never agreed to give his friend to the bounty hunter!

When Lando entered Han and Leia's cell to check on them, Leia asked him about their fate.

"He doesn't want you at all. He's after somebody called . . . uh, Skywalker. Lord Vader has set a trap for him," Lando explained.

"And we're the bait!" Leia exclaimed.

Meanwhile, Vader examined a massive carbon-freezing facility in the bowels of Cloud City. "This facility is crude," he said, "but it should be adequate to freeze Skywalker for his journey to the Emperor." But first, Darth Vader suggested that they test it . . . on Han Solo!

Moments later, stormtroopers marched Han, Leia, and Chewbacca—with C-3PO strapped to his back—into the carbon-freezing facility.

Han was moved into position and lowered into the chamber. Smoke billowed and hissed ominously, and Chewbacca howled in despair.

When the smoke cleared, Han was lifted from the pit. He was encased in a rectangular tomb of carbonite.

"He's alive, and in perfect hibernation," Lando said, relieved.

The stormtroopers took Han's frozen form over to Darth Vader to inspect.

"He's all yours, bounty hunter," Vader said. "Reset the chamber for Skywalker."

Darth Vader instructed Lando to take the princess and the Wookiee to his Star Destroyer. Again, Vader was changing the plan that he and Lando had agreed to. Lando feared that things were only going to get worse. He quietly signaled to his aid, Lobot. As Lando led the stormtroopers, Leia, and Chewie through the corridor, Cloud City's security guards quickly surrounded them.

"Well done," Lando said to Lobot, who had joined them. "Hold them in the security tower—and keep it quiet."

But as the guards took the Imperials away, Chewie lunged at Lando, choking him for betraying Han.

"There's still a chance to save Han," Lando said through strained breaths. "At the east platform . . ."

The group ran toward the east platform, but they were too late. Boba Fett had finished loading Han into his ship and flown away. But that would not be the end of Han Solo. His friends were already working on a rescue mission. All they had to do was escape from Cloud City—and Darth Vader!

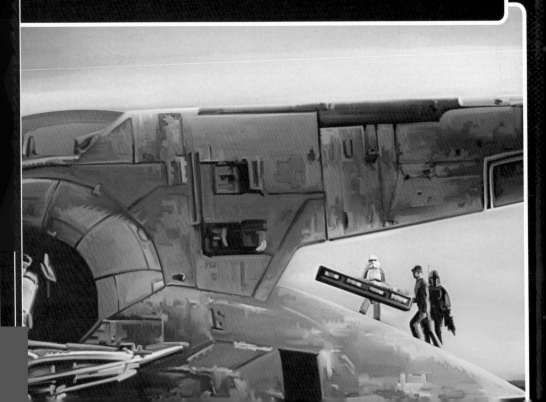